THE EVERY WILD

THE EVERY WILD

JD PLUECKER

M UTHFEEL PRESS

Contents

"What are you looking for?"
— The Ballet

". . .the experience of looking is deeper than the data accumulated. . ."
— Toni Morrison

THE EVERY WILD

A Note on Opening

Before we   begins then   to say we began inestimably long ago

arrived to this here disparate   impossible to congeal this we

yet lingers   an echo of that experimentalist

she said   if you enjoy it you understand it   so breathe and read aloud

everything flails   As we encounters the world in a perpetual confusion   invite

you   me   never quite knowing what or how to

how to integrate or comprehend

Know if just the slightest pressure   pleasure   if the most minimal stream

winds through muddy flat   defines underbrush   that synapses fire   connect

and how much sweetest to look and look   that goose skin   tremble

a beyond what we might formerly have called "understanding"

Some things do not quite make it across   the ford   born in refusal   end in nowhere

stubborn mules not quite to tell the story   she says   where is your body   or where is we

We is the swamp   becomes an operation of the middle   a cart abandoned

in bottomlands to degrade   a note not quite and yet a poem   or vice versa

even sunken or especially when stuck   a series of invented gestures

procedures   a means to forage through disorder

within things thingselves   a process to regard   report   cut and sculpt

look how things might fit unexpectedly   or elegantly   askew

this forever not quite to do the thing or   never document

the thing set out to document   rather to make another   a shell   neither

intended nor there originally   but a thing   to shimmer in the space

a glint in the gap   the brack

forever looking?   to look for that glimmer

We

Begins

this sister difficult on these
    words

                 neediness of
        waterways history   everything
        body the family   willing
                    gender be

slipped
        all   was   sensation flooding giant

                            marshes flowers   coast

                    glisten on   never

                        narrative
                        through
                        water   solid like words once

                            massaged my fear

                        your back brilliance
                                        beautiful

                                        sweet but

                            she be ordered

                        we of whore center
            sometimes something was   boom

            be lingering
            fingers aggressively deep
                        coming
                                        propping

                                        sensual

                                        as
                                        spindles of spider web

                  catch   an elbow
                  hug   the waist
                  leave   a mark

                                   is that sex

        can the name for one side   shaven green

 and one side   yellow wildflower

                         be border
                                    or   amaranthine

                  instead of the strain
                        to learn
                       the name
                  of a thing or its meaning
                  might it be

                              preferable

 to field

   to feed

 to felt

absence of demand

a just like   joyous   sensual
          occasion

                              unexpected

how to make   love to   ancestors
          take

                    despite
                         this very Empire
                              muscles in angles

               body stop
       acting
       like   descendant

               to receive benefit

                    while the decision of am

          a maximum desire
               unusual hormones

               pass   down
                 from daughter

                         to new daughter

                    ready the lashes

                              and legs
                    de-grated
          positioned
                    some
                    began
                         to lap
                              asshole
                                   as ancestor

                                                  mosquito welt
                                                  blooms

                                    a ring of transparent teeth

                                        crawl up the arm
                                        a hand in the rotting papaya

                        flesh lets the ants
              claim

        weekly crossdressing
    as practice

                                                one etymology of
                                                miniscule
                                          is error

                              the

                              self
                    but no matter

              dress of constant
                  transform a shun

                  earn faggot

                          locate

        how to write a recipe   with no
                      imperatives

                  and
            following
                  unnecessary

    somehow fruity

blue
jay   de-
                light

or blue jay
allows a sting

prehistory slavery
            future suture

and now
        two waters drop
        in palm

mottled   muddled textures

a john keeps   leaving

not Gayconnect
        being
                history
        chunk   an aggregate
pronouns replace

white cloud fluffs
                substitute
                referents
            supposedly understood
            "in context"
        but each
                one   hears   " "
        another   " "
                another   " "

                        referents spin
                spiral
                un-congeal

                        blue jay
                edges
                    tremble   in
                            the
                                brack

A Note on the Hooks

One year   I wrote poems with people I hooked up with

through apps on my phone   I'd hook up with people

and afterwards   I'd ask if I could read them a poem   They always said yes   I'd look

in my backpack or on the internet

for a poem that went with the vibe   and then I'd read it and

we'd talk   I'd take notes   I'd tell them the notes were for a poem I'd write later

After it was done   I'd offer the poem to the person   Sometimes

they wanted to see it   Sometimes

there were no humans available through the apps   I tried to work

through what it might mean to hook up with a non-human animal or plant

No matter the species   I'd read them a poem   All of these hooks in energy

Hook: Joseph

after reading from Joseph Brainard, I Remember

a retro 70s porn vibe dribbles
all over the bed   funk and a wave
of affection for all the fluffy
gray stuff with tiny red specks
inside your heart   for the two
and a half years on meth

my hand never stops skimming
the surface of skin   an Alabama beauty
queen ran off to Tasmania   dreams
of telling knock-knock jokes to blonde-
haired Australian surfers   The Cars
Janis Joplin Van Halen Black Sabbath
never shave to skin sky skip skills

dark poetry humps sexuality
in our thirties   admire the ragged
beauty of the elderly and no   you disapprove
of me   out of nowhere eating your ass
the way a baby's hand folds itself
round your finger   as though forever

upstairs bangs and thumps   the dog
sobs outside the door   we romanticize
bright lights silver instruments   exoticize
what is opposite   the humid South   the Turks
I'll get out of this desert   stoned
the most profound thought totally evaporates
whiteness as preference *and* supremacy

how silly it all seems   regular bowel movements
a perfect squat   knees behind the feet
perpendicular to the ground   paramount
pearls of cum betwixt beard hairs   feng shui
energy flows from back to front front to back
nibbles jumps   bassoon bassoon bassoon

contrabassoon contrabassoon contrabassoon
swirls off your tongue   I live under rhinoceri
or hippos   a dog still whining   tweakers
mean I'm not a people person but
yes that vagina is not boring
she really really let me have it   smiling

Hook: Dung Beetle

after reading from Luis Felipe Fabre, Escribir con caca

mierda mierda mierda I squat or you shat
out last night   who were you   animal?
caca caca caca   ¿qué me dices?   no casualty

faggots long time accustomed to this shit
packed beat down   shit shit shit shit shit   the gayz are known
by their shit   to shit   ashes to ashes   you little shit

I say affectionately   you tumble beetle
bumble with other bugs shat out night
before   globules of beetle masses shiny

striated textures   excreted beetles done
and come shit   I'm holing up with you
lean into you   crawl up my leg

penetrate with long proboscis
smear black dung into my forearm
suck on wings   my legs roll

we roll we roll we roll we roll
erotically significant   both fond and sick of the ground
rub shit into each other viciously

palmetto palm scrub oak cockroaches geckos
a collection of carapaces slopped on skin
man musk and pungency redolent   earth   I shit a million times a day

all of us you and me re-emerge re-digested   re-processed
words are caca and caca is life   you texted
either caca is sacred or this caca is all the things

black and deep like galaxies of blackness holes
holed up together   Kim Tallbear says if one thing is thought
sacred other things are thought not

so these colonizing languages are shit on tongues
no vocabulary for the existence of things
our relations the relations we make   shit!

the beetles embrace their dead and shout
decolonize your asshole!   decolonize your shit!
stuck on metaphors   I'm rolling around in bed with caca

tiny shreds of beetle carapace and wings
and legs and shit and cum   salty & musky
spread cheeks tiny hairs in the crack

never see the light of day
but the caress of your tongue or mine   yes
we can take turns   embrace debris

the shells of your devoured siblings   I eat you and I
don't know if this is cannibalistic
or sisyphean   tumblings   wrestling

with all your dead   these days anyone in touch with their anus
wrestles with all their dead   these
are days for grappling with cadavers   hay cadáveres

como dice Perlongher   ay mierda de los bichos   bichos raros nosotros
cogiendo a otros bichos raros y vomitando górgoros de mecos y
una poquita de mierda   una pesadilla   rough and vulgar   but no

be gentle girl   slow the fuck down   no shit is universal
all shit specific   beetle carcass compact
unlike any brother   you smear and I smear

if we can't be pretty   we'll be grotesque   and ludicrous   an anus
in our mouths and gawk   a tiny tea party   bacteria and infection the game
long time cumming   your bodies never been clean

the nurse advises   and that is a fearsome package   burrow
crawl mount   take it up inside backwards   reverse   pull it with your lips
devour it   all the shit sent our way   and we'll cum exorbitantly   re-emerge

caked   los amos nos van a envidiar nuestra entrega
the masters will envy us our devotion   our fearlessness   our gaping
shit   our tender   flower   caress

A Note on the Other Poems

A pandemic arrived and I stopped hooking up

At first   I didn't write much   Then a few months in   I began writing anew

sixty-four poems for the sixty-four ancestors from seven generations ago

those German settlers who first began to arrive to so-called Texas

I set myself very strict rules

me my own dom and most comfortable in restraints   each poem only sixty-four words

An entire year passed   and I did not hook up with humans   I came to feel

I was hooking up though   as in connecting   as in looking for

others in other ways   ancestors   ghosts   visible and invisible   begonias   snakes

swamps   my own body   mosquitos   randoms in Gayconnect.com chatrooms

the faces rectangled in Zoom   At first

I wrote the sixty-four poems alone

but then they began arriving in online writing spaces   workshops that blossomed

in that first year of the pandemic   I'd sketch notes   write and write and write   as CA Conrad

says   then sculpt those materials down to sixty-four words

excise all pronouns imperatives epiphanies   I am brutal with myself   I say

especially when   no one else will do the dirty work

Later   I stopped wanting to write those sixty-four poems of sixty-four words

The project sputtered   At that point   I had forty-two poems

Months passed   More months passed   I began to cut up the forty-two poems

to re-arrange the paper ribbons of text   to let them find

their friends   their own connections   their own ways to hook up

with one another   I forgot the rules or I let myself change the rules   to be my own dom

and to bottom for myself   All of these other poems are also hooks

in energy   bodies connect through desire   time   space

Return

Unsettlement

Fore   middle   background
     the camera   or the eye
pans across   depth of   banana leaves
   Spanish moss   begonia   snow down

          Thing is
                    worlding's so long been wrong
     re-do
          turn around   come back
     insist   A move
          Pauline Oliveros listens
                              as ever
               this body throws down
                              hole
                              from the
          wails
                    in fetal position
          wrap

     What is   a thing
          always returning
             to thingself?

                              A friend afar
     knows it isn't okay
                    but how is she not to awaken
     not to wrench   harder nor rouse
                         from kneaded sleep

Decades to re-learn   epigenetically
     how to re-root   in place   to re-main
             re-order   re-orient   re-make
          re-expressing intensive force

     brittle leavings of tomato   jalapeño

          dog days canícula   sun   burns

"The disconnection feeling is deep"
                    said the potted plant to the limp dick
                                        ecstatic   not lesser than

An artist friend   came to the house late
               clumped the pots into an altar
        prayer for the cut-out leaders to fall
                    paper slumps on the mantle
                                    into oyster mounds
        arrowheads   unseeded cede
               nothing   never consented
        rise murky   unencumbered

                                        For once
            the manager to be more troubled
                        than the waitress

        The clay says   "I know how to unsettle the settlement"
                            settle from the word sit
               meaning also re-concile   re-pair
               To re-ckon with sitting
        still   languages of intimacies
               intimates   signified
                        voiced or signs
        A clump   A knot of carrizo

            A spring whispers an earful
    inside   intimidation   timid
                    flows like a crystal creek through
               sand murmurs

    "Time is a shifting liquid"
               said Lorenzo Thomas
    "a shame / Nobody Understands /
                        shy"

            Summer   and the living is Gulf Coast
    okra   malabar   bananas   papayas

        Winter   on re-peat ushers
                    in gray and brown
            split sub-tropical drapery
    In Bay City a horizon   a line of cut paint
               the same knife Forrest Bess used

                    to open a portal
                                    in his body   our bent future

        Ritual   Cecilia Vicuña says   a manner to stop
                                                      or pause a
            reminder   water spurts
                        gush

    An altar wrapped in perished leafery   A shack toppled
                to the marshes   A screen
        array of   perfectly arranged   grounds

            A time   as ever   for
                            well-aimed undercuts

Hook: JonJon

after reading from Jericho Brown, *Please*

the rigidity
this is red and it is forever red
what if I walk into a gallery
and call pink black   what does it even mean
to be blue
tailoring

oh post coital poetry
a slender man wanked in
and told me   take it   you said
especially with the law   deep inside
the gay who brought poems
is afraid of colors
intimacy

a masters in colors   Oscar
Wilde made a painting of a book
and Whistler sculpted layers of paint
black doesn't exist   you said either it's red warm
or cold blue
temperature

the bitch is high
one day it hit me   that's not green
it's yellow   you are colorblind
only in amiss   well you gave me a load
I'll give you
poems

the law is an ocean
smooshed into a cup   the law doesn't exist
I say it so many times you vomit
the law doesn't exist
the law is always
evolving to inflection
and the girl they're making fun of
is me

I have just picked up a man
and I am afraid he'll talk
disarm me with a smile
poetry is more fun
than just leaving
you failed the colorblind test   you said
I aced it

Hook: Hugo and the Moss

after reading Emily Dickinson, "Poem 1400"

r u cut or uncut?   the mosses and me
pre-programmed texts   looking?   maybe
u?   LOL   into?   being afraid and sometimes
awkward   looking to suck   LOL   poppers?

wanna cum over here?   argh
another gentrified swath of townhomes
or palmetto palm paradise
the door unlocked   moss in the air

I'm on my knees   waiting
cum in cum over   it'll be a dream
my head on moss pillow
legs splayed in the air   you mossy

sperms legion and desired
we traffic sex   you insect
my infection traffics in sex
my sex insect or masc?

do not appear afraid   honestly   I'm into
470 million-year-old bryophytes
your asexual anti-dick   the sweat
drips off my glasses   into your eyes

emit volatile compounds all over the knees   kneel
to the ground   kneel townhome
kneel   to pity that I know her not
to suck the spores out of thee

and yet we flip   the same species and oh
mossy   seven micrometers tower   you are
stranger   yet nature   floorless
AC whirs   aeroplane contrail   we fake clean

moss and I   and you and moss and
we is a townhome 470 million years ago   we climbs out
the swamp   drenched in moss sperm
into a moist corner   masked

my mask masc?   enough   only
insects sex this sex   moss
brown & subtropical crawls
up stucco or stuck to rot

wood   my own thighs   your chest
hair a carpet of moss   I burrow deep
wood and wood and wood til your completion
no recip   what lies

We

Begonia

A begonia I grew from cuttings

given to me by my dad   given to him by his mother   Hertha

who lived in a house blocks away from me

in this same East End

by the confluence of the bayous so-called Brays and Buffalo

bayou ghosts   begonia ghosts

                              toppled
        gravestones
                  for minor

          figures
unremembered   dismembered yet
                        present

                  absences

                        abscesses
                            pus oozes

This is a family of becauses

   the confusion caused by being
       in flower
    how dangerous the grip in intestines

       borders supposed to produce
        self-portrait
     identity what was pulled
             but it it

       is focus   is future

         the history
          when the humidity
             came inside

    Mimi says everything is in the blood

     but that liquid is hardly exactly one
          anymore

      a globe looks upon
   a tree   versus   a non-tree

  "There is always something genealogical about a tree"

        cut the visible branches

       self a decision?
       as we preens

        a time for muffled

          whistling
         preen baby

                                        Begonia treasure
                         mistaken
                     for centuries

        undoes fantasy   ordered thinking
            boundaries

                     these leaves
                              this caudex
            did not birth

                a flower genus

                   a set of tepals
                incarnate
                        the passage

    written in breath   botany butchers

                  photocopied tree
            a drawing

                          froze this
                          "study of descent"

                               the lie in
                ancestral trunk: two individuals
                              multiplied by
                                   descendants
                          spindle
                                   imagination beyond
                                        a finite
                                     order

        other potential structures
            for genealogy:

                aphids under leaf   okra stalk-born
                 cum on the floor   society garlic
                own cloud-being   bastard children
                      odor   begonia caudex

Rhizomes not roots

some rhizomatous begonias

Begonia acetosa
                    Begonia bowerae
                        Begonia 'Bow Nigra'

            Begonia 'Buttercup'
                        Begonia 'Cleopatra'
                                Begonia 'Crestabruchi'

Begonia goegoensis
                Begonia 'Joe Hayden'
                        Begonia manicata
                                    Begonia prismatocarpa,
                Begonia rajah
                        Begonia 'Tiger Kitten'
                            Begonia 'Universe'

                        Begonia versicolor

To believe in the versicolor

A metal pole juts
        from earth
a blue plastic cord
                wound three times
                                the papaya trunk
                pulls it
                from one side
                                upright

                a white stick
                pushes

                        from the left

If the tree is to
        survive another winter
                on this overheated chemical coast

                green fruits
                might
                        ripen again
                                to sweet
                dribbles

                        Hope is

                active doubt
                        a not-knowing

        what comes
        blooms

        flowers will
                to open
                        for bees arrive
                                cyclical yet friab

Oh, Deleuze and Guattari

       philosophized
     rhizomes   a common place

perhaps   but not just
    a redoubt for the elite

  so:
"The rhizome is reducible neither to the One nor the multiple

      It is not the One that
        becomes Two or even directly three four five etc.

   It is not a multiple
     derived from the One   or to which One is added
                       $n + 1$
         It is composed not

        of units but of dimensions
             or rather directions

       in motion

      It has neither
     beginning nor end
        but always a middle
            milieu

     from which it grows

   and which it

        overspills"

Anglos want
a fake
roots

or oh no   genealogy means stability   or here the feeling won't
for   the
sake
of
its own

Every history see say please

how to people-please

undresses
out of the dress
to be included

forgets the most basic of recipes

Is it even a recipe without the imperatives?

Demanding Grandma Hertha gave
a line
what a line
feels
as more than
passing lie

mean?
mean.
mean!

a season to peter out
or how a human arrives to end the season

not prematurely
but recognizes the cleavers
splay forth

and without the recognition

does the season exactly end

The genus name *Begonia*

was coined by Charles Plumier,

a French patron of botany   and adopted by Carl Linnaeus in 1753

to honor Michel Bégon

a former governor of the French colony

of Saint-Domingue (now Haiti).

The family tree is

       all the phantom limbs
         the dreamed ones

                what is that sissy tree

                  its crown sweeps
              through the mess
                        of sky

                      Nacogdoches
                          to stop at a cemetery

                  Where's Papa's grandma?

              Wilhemina Rimmele
                or
              Mina R. Pluecker

                  an erasure
              a run through gravesites

      How are all these people

                Muñoz
              González
              Voigt

                    whether plastic flowers
                      or degraded nineteenth century

        letters blur into moss and mold and stone

                    how is all is this
                    not family
                who lived here together
             and decompose each day
                  in the same soil

Oh, *Bonds of Alliance:*
          Indigenous and Atlantic Slaveries in New France:

"Bégon synthesized existing law and practice

          into a sixteen-page memorandum ˅
containing dozens of provisions for slave management

               Sent to Versailles in February 1683
                              Bégon's memoir became

     with only a few minor adjustments

the first comprehensive slave code in the French Caribbean

     and one of the most influential bodies of slave law
        in the early modern world"

                              Bégon

               ↓   ↓

          Begonia   Code Noire

Just stop
                like stop
        like when did   no

permanent disaster zone
                        refreshes thousand-fold

focus   she says again

                imagine   mom
                        takes the house apart

                slowly

instead of adding on
                gives everything back

        or
                a thousand
        worms try to worm
                their way
                        through the rot

like isn't there a memory there

                                                looking

                for the initial injury
                        that set all this
                                this in motion

        like stop   just stop

                        like when did   no

The begonia doesn't get to be

simply a flower

It is not a flower   not a plant

It is

                              stain passes down

                                        with word on word in
                    word

                         the Black Code is the plant
                                   as it is cut
                                          re-potted
                                        transported
                         bloomed

               and still   damn
                                 no way to un-name
                                      everything

Oh, Deleuze and Guattari:

"There is no mother tongue   only a power takeover

      by a dominant language
           within a political multiplicity

          Language stabilizes

       around a parish
          a bishopric
        a capital

               It forms a bulb

          It evolves by subterranean stems and flows

       along river valleys or
            train tracks

         it spreads like a patch of oil

             It is always possible to break"

My dad never could tell me what kind of begonia

he gave me

But I found the kind online in pictures   Begonia "Joe Hayden"

                              Oh, Begonias.org:

                    "Mr. Hayden was an early Begonia member
                              who retired and lived in Vista   California

                    We had a little contest
                              to see who could find the darkest
                              leaved rhizomatous begonia

                    In his working life
                              he was an Englishman

                    who went out from London on to the colonies
                              establishing motion

                                        picture

                                        theaters

                                        in the early days."

How to divide self
    into 64   or 128

    pot-bound roots
     coil endlessly

        breathe in
        breathe

          "The rhizome is an anti-genealogy"

            a contradiction

              "but"
                postures defensive

     Of course   the begonia is tarnish too
              is
           patriarchal map

                 white
                   as
                    a wave good-bye

                         how to expand
                      present moment

                         a prophecy
                 floor undersea
                      changes the storm

               above is the rage   amidst the particular

                  still and still
                    sunken
                 on that floor
                  the wreck
                   a loss of
               navigation
               yet still persists
                 in still-
                    ness

Oh, *Popular Mechanics:*

"Light itself actually slows down as it barrels

through the Begonia plants› chloroplasts

due to the precise arrangement of the tower-like thylakoids

which together act like a dense crystal

While light always travels the same speed

in a vacuum, it will slow down
when passing through different types of matter

what is known in quantum physics as

slow light"

                    the woman in the back
              shadows
        says a thing
                    such a long time ago

no one remembers
                    what was lost
years passed for sound to travel
                    was everything

        angry children
                    light the family
        tree aflame

the bright lit faces

                    christmas
        birthday party
                    summertime

each generation's

                    camera
        registers lightness
                    as presence

        an array of blurs
        and dark faces

              the erasure multiplies

              no end

              to this delighting

How to dig up the roots when,

oh, Édouard Glissant

      "the root begins to act like a rhizome

            there is no basis for certainty

         the relation is tragic"

But turmeric
        undried leaf and stalk
          wind-collapsed

                    today a stomach knot
                            or for the better part of a year

        products of little import

                  stomached
                      or did stomach

                            was ground
                  what emerged

                          their rhizomes orange and sexy

          A snail spiral of prospering
                            protuberances penetrate soil

              soil penetrating organic folds
                        on   the   of   other pathway

                          a mound
                              for how growth

                                to be a phrase in
                                  waxing

                  when the little bulb
                            emplaced

                            a-rockets
                        spurts

Oh, Glissant:

". . .a reconstituted echo or a spiral retelling. . ."

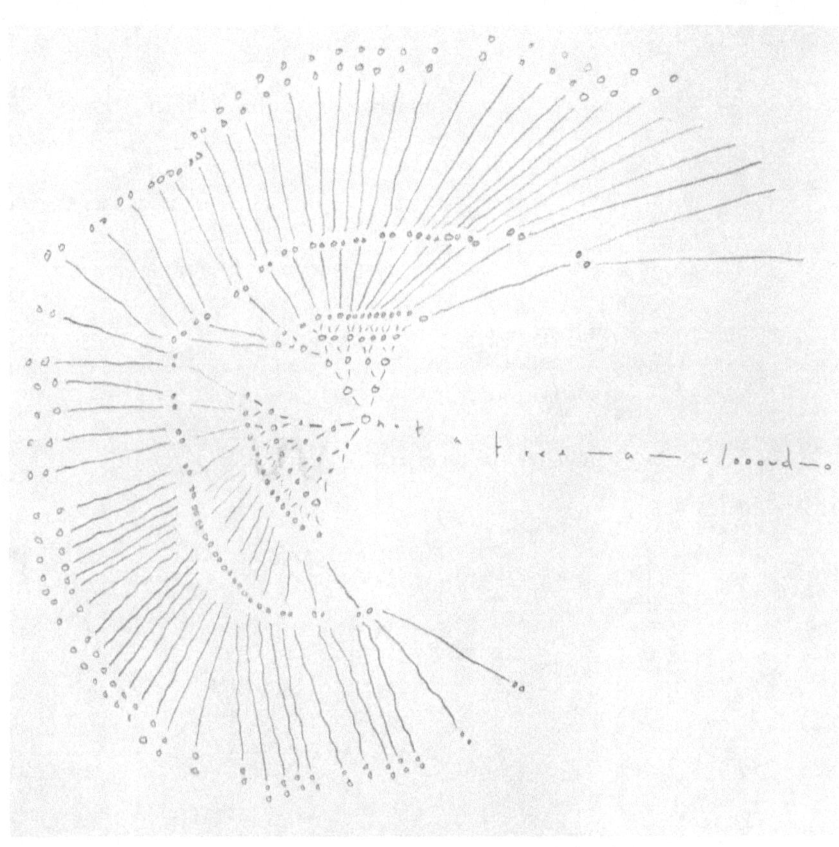

Who we is for one another
     cut

          scars
            along the curve
      of
        thigh

               a hand
                    pockmarked
          with nicks and cuts

                    of unremembered origin

                              Two rabble rousers
                                  say no
                    to a list of in-
                              appropriations: throw down   dope   flex

               who was cut   who does the nicking

                    courage   versus   fragility

          is there a map
               online
           of hurt

      inflicted and received

                    how to search

               an index   of
                                   escalation

               What if the we

                         begonia

                         to lover the fallen branch

Hook: Alejandro
después de leer / after reading Julio Serrano Echeverría, "Piedra caliza"

el espacio hueco
también fue piedra

the hollow space
was also stone

todo hueco nace
de una partida

every hollow is born
of a splitting

el hueco es transformación
río montaña y mar

the hollow is transformation
river mountain and sea

el hueco con miedo esconde
hundido en agua salobre

the hollow with fear is hiding
sunk in the brack

partir el hueco en dos
volverlo habitable

split the hollow in two
render it habitable

una lumbre se enciende
en la roca   en un hueco

a fire is lighted
in the rock   in a hollow

acabar venir terminar
el hueco varía   intraducible

finish come end
the gap varies   untranslatable

o el acto se termina
cuando uno se olvida

or the act ends
when one forgets

o el olvido ya es la esperma
sobre una mano abierta

or forgetfulness already is the sperm
on an open hand

se va   y hueco   le dicen   pero
insiste   continúa   echa raíces

one leaves   and hollow   they call her
but insists   continues   drops roots

penetra la superficie
escarba huecos en lo hondo

penetrate the surface
dig hollows in the depth

hueco   una palabra
que se propaga   y

hollow   a word
that propagates herself   and

hueco   el que la mire
y la lea

hollow   the man who watches
and reads her

A Note on We

over a long term there comes to be a we

we comes

to enforce certain grammatical patterns

bodies to fit semantically into a series of weeks

and months   call that we a family

or couple   partners   lovers   leaves

siblings   hooks   friends   readers   weeks and months

become years and generations and continually

subject verbs object   subject verbs object   subject verbs object and long term is a series of sentences where the subject becomes fixed

along with its verbs and objects

and a family tree is a series of lines to fix the subjects

into an arboreal we that verbs its objects

we becomes a series of sentences strung together   where the one

only makes sense because the one

before has preceded one   we thinks one understands

even as we doesn't   I was born here but grew up elsewhere   for example

grammar is a structure like a sapling in need of continual unrooting

to set down roots   the shepherd's hand massages soil so aeration allows growth

and unrooting is a story told or untold   well-folded

An undercut is surgical   fleshy   undermines   topples

So this is not a memoir   we is dealing with official knowledge   absorbs aspects

she asked   but how to do that without it getting more oxygen

than it has already taken?

and because we so deeply imagines how the upcoming sentences will play out we knows or we out-stretches

narratives into past and future

should we resist an idea   stories that must be told   the seduction of story

storytelling to undo the dominant story told   or we undone   M. Nourbese

Philip "Only in not-telling can the story be told"

how does we let each member be one

we asks ourself

how does we imagine every day   to render ourself surprising   present

also as in gift   a present   How does we let our sentences re-new   re-create

and we generations and generations lay interwoven

under sheets   stained

covered with cums   plural in that other foreign language

that makes this language foreign   also something unknown and pleasant

and some of that energy

arrives to previous phrase

comes on we   begonia

we insists on speaking othered tongues

across boundaries   old new tongues entirely

we finds ways to support a move

into old new grammars   piece together alternate clauses

out of old new alphabets and sketch characters   What can be fabricated out of this

something unknown and pleasant   of this   what is known already or the languages

in which already   or this between-language that is   as they all say

you both talk exactly the same   you the same as your great-great-grandmatriarch

and your gaylover

and your sister   History is continually made to be coherent

but present this rupture   the constant disturbance of timeline

a repetition of circles   what has we come looking for   a hook up   a lick

an apology   an impossible expungement   and it's true how phrases have interlaced

but   still there are those times

when we slips

What does we make of this something unknown   or misknown and pleasing

of this what we knows or the tongues in which already we has moved

these mounds   Gulf Coast oyster mounds   fabricated into Modernist concrete

re-fabricated by Jamal Cyrus into a triangle   paired with sargassum

laid on the floor   Difficult to know   what is our MO

or where one narrative ends

and the other begins   Where to place the comma   or how to maybe add

three spaces there   a red wolf in Galveston become a canid   because we has come togethe

we has provided an array of options that we is always looking

at   but now that we is not in the same common place

we stops or

pauses   or we tries out old new grammatical shifts learned

from other lovers   other town squares or histories

that fallen branch

other syntactical structures or variances to enliven

deadened dead-end sentences   lines   branches

not always just go go go   on to the next

no no not

we finds a ritual to pressurize the moment

or we is constantly pulling things or thinging the pulls

she asks   How do you not make something

that is just a clever queer version of a space they already know   We constantly

things the pulls in new ways   some things some one's said

during the day become hooks for we

your adventures or mine   We likes how it makes our structures public   our slip-ups

life is not a series of line breaks or fragments   or it is

about narratives as joinings of clauses into sentences

a string of sometimes independent but more often subordinate clauses

subordinated look to find a way to join up

and the struggle to do so   and how the run-ons keep on

running on

dependent narratives intertwine   so "quite obviously" it does not "make sense"

to suddenly make just one moment the way that hooks are one moment

or no   sense is the least important thing   Stress in English is not natural

she says   not like the thump thump thump of your heart

bassoon bassoon bassoon   contrabassoon

contrabassoon contrabassoon

the indeterminate we has made a way to string sentences

to take a subject and verb it

and then object   object our way into another verb   the way things unfit

thingether   always askew

old new structures allow new old structures to lean

collapse   relax   we breathes in an old new way

our coming together

object verbs subject   verb objects subject   object subjects verb

all of we   endlessly   comes

Hook: Eric and the Bees

after reading from Renée Gladman, *Calamities*

failure can be a hook
blows up all the magnolia
grenades   queen commerce

headless and golden af
strap on pounds
humans pack bees in slits   head

north or west   alfalfa almonds
overproduced   mechanized   longing
manscapes of bottoming

forehead   brush of sweaty pubes
queens mate   with 15 or 16 drones
doggy style   use less   monsanto   bayer

gmo jelly for passive penises
you drive to pollinate   gorge on
loveliness   everything textured letter by

let her pounce to splay
nausea reels   blueberries sappy
cherries bears   laurel and water oak stares

all night long   ass got shimmered
so damn good   three guys and mangrove's
honey but here alone   molten bi extremities

Hook: Phil

after reading Kathy Acker, "The Diseased"

fuck u and your Rupaul-loving stepdad
would make a good   banana earlier

and a yogurt and apples a meal bananas are a meal lets go
tacos or pizza   you only said the word once

and that was enough to warp our flogging   we never say the word
just keep wailing away   all the new spoons and spatulas blood and guts cancer

we're not fucking anymore I let slip   I got fat and he works out constantly
a fish slips from the monger's hands   flaps on the tile

a bin of sad brown frogs   yes you're a little racist but that's not the only reason I'm
here   a BDSM anthology   no one is buying what they're selling

I'm hungry   I want something other than our men miles away
we fake fats and femmes will play   love's more powerful than social climbing

diseased trails and 10 miles or 40 miles   the hurricane fucked it all
up my thighs thick drip horny or flick not horny he   never horny anymore

it was just the anniversary of my parents watching Ru every
say   smart plug connected to the Wemo   Wifi up and running

hey Google its sexy time   hey Google let's get it on
no that's not what I want   hey Google turn off all the lights

Can you wallop the weirdly bro-y sickness out of me
dribbles down my chin   wall-to-wall carpeting

When I was a kid   you all wanted nothing to do with it
but now you call me   ask about the most recent episode

I haven't even seen yet   because Rupaul
is the only gay thing I do anymore   and that hardly ever

Return

Gayconnect

One night it it it was oceans   was point beautiful
     repeat three times
                              this man and the wide steppes

               saliva brilliance to expose
          screen
     Finger slipped in vehemently

               computer pink entry

     a chat the eye   two of the anus
effaces   the
                    shame   The man's props   his
                                        exposed inside

               to awaken
     emotional perineum
                                   How does slip slip?
          slip out of which conjuring world?
                              This Gayconnect?
                                   This chat?

     A finger
               before sprouting center
                    pleasure at this orifice tongue says
          now
               tongue says
                    mine Black Sea

     to cute from lower pop skin attractive

A Burn Book
                        maybe gay tone or the wing
fungus on the log
        spurts over a mud
    a bath   A spiky white rain
                            can't land   its landing

    is bumpy   damage

            hope   a diptych   is

        still in there?
                    alive? alive

unsettlement is no hierarchical hand-out

            hand arrives nowhere
        non-line

    blossoms a flower of repose

                to ignite

                        aflame

Burn! A burn! Cut cut cut!
            A Catholic nightclub is   yeah
    always "his" terrain   ugh   pleasure
            in just not   y'know?

teeth up licking inserting positioning

                                        mouth

        from Latin
    "manus" meaning   "hand"
        plus
"turbare" meaning   perhaps
            "to unsettle   to throw into disorder"

        Language this
        wordsound
                    grates   and   defiles
                        the un-master

        hand-unsettle
        or hand-re-throw-re-order

    a definition can be   an attack
                    so away with

                    instead

what if   no interior

just folds   no end

happy limp penis in
                              desert sands
                    fingers coil a circle
two rounded moons
                    sway lavish   undulate
          fingers gesture toward long lashes
          impish smile

          two faces
          legs akimbo
with the metropolitan pronunciation now
                              "bien"

Overnight it it it was oceans   was point beautiful

          like recognize   glorious finger orifice

          a thumb up
          another finger
          slides in

          a riot of passives
          and escape
                    desire
a mouth opens and closes
          a tongue protrudes rhythmic

          a spatter
          a smile

          a lips slicked

Hook: Eduardo

after reading Julian Talamantez Brolaski, "on loneliness"
y después de leer Jaime Sabinas, "Los amorosos"

Los amorosos refuses to be translated
not lovers   not plural   certainly not coupled
the loving ones maybe or we the loving   not compromised
the mistranslation   purposeless   no full   you noticed
we are uncommitted
to perfection

a turn on made of arousal   disallowed
or you refuse to turn on   the hook over
before it began   nothing like chastity as threat   rush blood to extremity
the loving seek   silence   silence
forget how puddles linger
never

evaporate   you want the sea at our side
constantly   only the flood waves do not worry   lap the sand bags
perhaps the affectionate   traverse forest floors   parallel personhoods
a slick retort   no control   in this occurrence
if you and I never cum thingether
I'll be upset

you say   and I turn on   brakes or you are careful
about ceding power or   I am still so afraid of my own
body   age   a new iteration   primordial faggoty flaw   ill be upset   I say
or I've already lied   one day   we'll ride
or I'll whimper   elderly
can climb trees

ride them   all in parallel   and we hides
like   thick crowns of leaves   obscure tongues
summon resolve   a soft insistence   education of sentiments   like culturing
poetry but   in deeping gape caverns
before letters
and you

like I   will only top   with backside convincing
not a day less   not an allowance   oh you are unloving
if it rains   let it pour   dry ground   yield and flex   its pores   soaking   with whatever
soil has craved most   you cut me down to size   I don't want you
I does   to dice me smaller   paradoxically   bits
entitlement

with no place in the bedroom
you demand   Travel is like death in that
it requires mourning   you'll leave   be quickly evacuated   disinflated   silence   silence
fear becomes   the light   nerves   fingertips   I lay back   I feel waves   lap trains
muddy pheromones   rush   I *feel* the sounds
in the other room

the plants   their inexplicable wilting
in 1996 the poet says   love is   a perpetual deferral
a persistent postponement   an eternal extension   an insistent lingering   el poeta lo dice
in one   I offer four   and keep offering   as always
mistranslations
ride

like wind over land
bare   smooth   unexpected   you extend
wait   or we delay   everything   the cheek finally   appreciated
surface-oriented
untouchable
this

Swamps
Fly

(The photos in this section were taken by me

of sculptures made by Elana Mann

for her exhibition *Sounds from the Swamp* at Lawndale Art Center in 2020)

What if

    the jungle and swampy woods
       cleared and drained

        drench the abuses

          puddles studded with striders

            a shadow where the moon once was

               What if things
                  unlivable?

            Please
              stagnant water
                    speaks
             always
                 susurrates under canopy

           tambourine rattles
                like flat crack

            trouble ground
         despite an everything

                   to beneath bayou
                   to naming from cargo
                   to chirp dying city
                     to halloing the wasteland

                   not better-than

                    not clean or

                  marshes to be
                     ever

                  impure

James Audobon: "We landed at Houston, the capital of Texas, drenched to the skin [...] The Buffalo bayou had risen about six feet, and the neighboring prairies were partly covered with water; there was a wild and desolate look cast on the surrounding scenery."

dreams wetten
          to land

        the instruments
                listen calmly

            corpulent
            scattered
        over volcano

        ground flat
                distracted sounds

                        overwonder

                    What to hardly earth experience
                    honor our every wild

                        a steamer
                            grounds
                              the
                            warts

                        family trees and family
                            begonias

                    One could picture
                        a none more difficult topic

                        not

                    liquidy recalcitrant
                        that quagmire

                    imaginary

                entranceway being the good

                    colonized ungentle settler
                            bronzes
                            again

This phoneme morass
          remembers

               under the murmurs
                         malaria
                    and mosquito
                    research
                 through
          earthen layers
             pierce
                settler strip mall linoleum
                (this outside of place)

               This coast now
                    improved

                    became concrete plain
                         unbearable?

                              mulch
                                   hum
                                   lower
                              all by law

                    Allen bodies
                    still manage
                         settlement

                    let more to
                         create to
                    support spread of

                    swamps fly
                    off
                         to discover who

                    to find
                              another

Vittoria Di Palma in *Wasteland: A History*: "The nature of the Fens is neither to be entirely wet, nor dry, but is rather to be an indeterminate, recalcitrant, muddy mixture, constituting a landscape that is unsettlingly, gloriously, and permanently 'out of place.'"

a sound

      lake
        a   frog
      under the roar of cars

  many of black ooze
        back
      open
        as swirlgrass

            not
          1836
          founder responsibility disease

            descendants
          to live in relation to a damage
            rice reservoir
               re-made as park

     could the morass
       be long in an archive

        flooding and molded
          hipswerves

               ink on yellowed paper

                eludes   illusion
             violent falsehood
              paper not root but re-process

                    scanned

                        risen

                    pitifully
                      unsettlingly

                  scumming

To daughter
        meltdown at the sign
                insect bites
                        zika
                        ratsnakes

                                landed the steamer
                furnished
                        neighboring prairies ponded a
                        mess unraveled

                        transformed

                                        The water
                                senses the good
                                        mud decorations
                        a city ever a green scummed lake

                                What
                                        alligators
                                                spirit there
                                                        is swamp
                                        to let in and who
                                        wrote to do what

                        drenched to the skin
                                oyster mound parking lots
                                        research
                        settler eradication

                dream
                        the bayou
                                circular
                        womb-like
                maternate

O.F. Allen in *The City of Houston from Wilderness to Wonder*: "One could hardly picture the jungle and swampy woods that a good portion of the city is built upon. These swampy grounds had to be cleared and drained. The writer himself quite clearly remembers that the southwestern portion of the city was a green scum lake, studded with giant sweet gum trees, and water from one to two and a half feet deep... The labor of clearing the great space was done by negro slaves and Mexicans, as no white man could have worked and endured the insect bites and malaria, snake bites, impure water, and other hardships. Many of the blacks died before their work was done."

daughters
                array
      cross shallow black
                    plashes

      slight clear creek
            whines through leafmass

            O that the Bayou
                        was
                      once

                  a sound
                    a drumbeat from subordinate

      shimmer in grand sheets
            through sunken ranch-style living rooms
                  lower

                        than the road

            rose up like a white   rage
                  no response
                        ability

                  a will un-wrought   but not in hand

            the marsh
      steady steady bubbles
            asunder

            before on such occasion

                  to unforget

Find the bison
        water Buffalo
            cicada humming

        What was that sound
                in the brush

        listed alligators
    daughter
            stumbling about
                treaty
                decorations

            Wasteland lies

        like a lazy evening before

                    the big arrived
        contamination

        white as metaphor

                does not
                    endure
                        the enslaved

        gotta wear the spirit

            from the beginning of the day

            sweet gum trees
                water
            be but where

These
    swamps
        stay afraid

                this blackness constituting

                        a
                        depth
                            of

Frank A. Perret in *What to Expect of a Volcano*: "The strongest of impressions ... was, for the writer, that of an infinite dignity in every manifestation of this stupendous releasing of energy. No words can describe the majesty of its unfolding, the utter absence of anything resembling effort."

A weary ecosystem
        litters memory

    a hand cupped at the base

                    for what knew

                            to
                              be
                                afraid

        yes   daughter
              sees
    nature in concreted unswamp
            (above the scenery
            thoughts muddy)

        What a deep

                claiming

            to trouble

    waterways this heaven
        this stubble in the answer

                stores
                    dirt alive

        the floodplain
                    finds

            birds   chirp chirp chirp

    again
            descendant of all creatures
                living along

                    as Lisa Harris trills

                "all day long

            til the day goes away"

Return

So Many

so many this mornings so many movement so many breezes
so many cypress so many doorways demolished so many brush
so many vines crawl up the front of that house and so many
spaces so many wide open between one structure and another
so many ditches so many cars parked in the grass in front of a home
supposedly abandoned where people live so many branches
piles at the curb so many beat-downs so many row houses
gone and so many porches so many cut-throughs so many feeling
still in the wood so many highways invade so many train horns
blow softly so many autumn morning so many springtime dusk
so many pink afternoon as the sun peeks through the blinds so many
pick-up trucks so many suvs so many milk factories and so many
18 wheelers so many tiny plastic bottles of milk and so many oaks
and so many farms and so many concrete and so many cracked
and so many peeling paint so many thickness so many depression
so many joy so many angry pinpricks so many back-ups so many
give me a hug so many late night drunken driving so many early
morning so many mourning doves so many cooing so many police
sirens so many listening so many humans walk the middle of the road
so many cars wait to pass so many anger and so many smile so many
apprehension so many thistles so many concrete slabs so many gape
so many lost and so many nights so many grandmas so many grandkids
so many people just trying to remember what used to be there
so many new people who just got here so many things to misremember
so many escape memory so many brains so many bodies so many
bodies gone and so many cemeteries marked and unmarked so
many ditches so many huevo con papa and cake so many deep
deep breaths so many sighs so many pauses so many moments of
silence so many marches so many meetings god so many meetings
so many attempts so many failures so many new townhomes so many
dispossessed so many carwashes so many cowboy hats so many persons
forced out so many barbecues so many coolers so many bags of ice so
many country ballads so many accordions so many quiet so many loud
so many noisy so many silent so many germans so many telephone road
so many lasagna so many pupusa so many gordita so many jaywalker
and so many dance moves at the bus stop so many jiggling and so many
cars pass by so many stares and so many awkwardness so many
good mornings so many fuck you's so many fights and so many love-
making so many graffitied so many murals so many old doors so many

lintels so many country people come to the city so many bulldozers
and so many work crews so many dusty lifts into air so many hardhats
and so many pallets so many pine and so many sheet of metal
so many buses so many stray dogs so many mean-mugging
and so many evictions so many eminent domain so many minimizing
and so many excuses so many money so many reasons so many justify
so many sadness so many let it go and so many so-called misunder-
standings so many moldy and wet so many floodlines so many hurricanes
so many attitudes so many perspectives so many sung and un-sung so
many panaderías demolished so many pushing and so many pulling
so many mechanics so many broken down cars so many lay in the sun so
many wait so many trees blow in the early morning wind so many
speed up and so many people go home so many people go to work so
many undone so many bulldozers so many hoses spray water on wreckage
so many shovelfuls of metal and lumber so many precious objects discard so
many lost in the tumble so many feelings so many yellow and red so many
silver and gold so many blue and green so many green things so many grass
so many suns beat down so many heatstrokes so many city moves on
so many layers so many accumulations so many things a street a street remember

A Note on Looking

Look   slower now   slow down   eggshell   slow down

between what I is looking for and the experience of looking

to return   And to endlessly arrive and realize

what I was looking for   beyond the gates into despondency   beyond gerunds or roots

or meetings or assholes or community or dicks   Hey   Hi   Lookn?   looking for you

and I constantly looks across

creates a reality of tearing tearing   a different

sounding   against an unreal world   but they just might be happy   you know

what I was looking for was description   to describe and thus to feel

it   real   and I looks back into the past to see the story of I's arrival

to re-write the fit   or to engage with its fictions and all the loss   the grief of arriving a

I is not trying to be confusing on purpose   but yes to realize

the divides   without immediately hustling a "we" in the aftermath

A finger points up to the sky as if something were there

the cloud   another whitecloud   a darkcloud droops

Look! and every kid looks   something is there   under   the long   wait

everything's   weight   untrustworthy I fucks I's way across a series of applications

of theory in the world   I as useful   and I engages I's own absence

arrives to thresholds of betterment   arrives apocalypse   dream a bleek

the back of being not berth   birth banana pups   poke up

in alliteration or was it phenomenon

a posititional   libidinal   identification   attachment   cut eyes across

the space between you and object

WYD

NMU?

and how to read   and how to organize a meeting

or to get the women and children to safety

Lookn?   another spelling   an other mood   lookn is not looking

Lookn as in here ready to please lookn to give lookn to be judged   severely

lookn to serve lookn for approval   lookn for verbal a King   endowed kings

relish self-obsession   muscle worship   I offers a workshopped frailty   a we-

akness   but anesthetized   royals   do fascism

is this a temporary   sensation

knocked   blacked out   blanked out

yes I is here and ready and urgently DTF   how embarrassing

after the storm at the bar buying a round for everyone

and I want you to be here with me now   I is all ready to do this

to be looking is to be ready   for an other to arrive who might just be an other

I   a mirror   I is open to whatever   a blank slate   no dear   what

What are *you* into?

Look!   away from the phone and at the land   this is a neighborhood

by a graveyard   by the oil derrick   by longhorn   a beloved underused park

overused cruising ground of Black cowboy descendants

you and I wandered in to find

a nineteenth-century family cemetery   a decapitated baby doll

what are we looking for?   attacked by a swarm of mosquitos

and fleeing a high-walled tunnel of vegetation   oh the drapery of hundreds

of golden-orb spider webs   high and low and surrounded and we scream

sternum flares   chest open

heart stops   blood pump

plastic veins   light exists nonetheless   clearly the experience of looking wilder

than the data accumulated

the sun shines through   all these spiderwebs

at the same goddamn time

image returns   upon the eyelid dark   to the eyes

eye is looking   gains other meanings   a moment for   slow the fuck down

use the image   look   in real time

hark!   a subject watches their phone in a hotel room   during quarantine:

two lanes   slope down   cut cross caked

grassy plain   like miniatured   left   stubby trunks

hazy   out of focus   rounded

details   leaf and crowns

cirrus streaks   blue   hours

from destination excised   Wanna play?

she is already gone

a solid square refusal   I vanishes again

ashamed   so much sex in shame   the point   blank

A row of seventeen open gates   floats in context-less space

or tabs   or furrows   the difference between a painting and an image on the phone

looking at "a very good painting" she wrote

a photo would be the same? what is it about it being "very good"?

what is in the picture   doesn't need to be written   she says

what is seen is not questioned   no that's not the translation   it is

not to be questioned   what is visible   doesn't need to be described

or so I translated   and then I becomes visible to I   at least in the other's eyes

I's own   yet some see but do not look

and thus these things require   description   no?   repetition

on repeat   to describe the sin-

mplest thing   repeat   repeat   repeat

add to that no: a refusal to spill   into underbrush gaps

What I end up looking at is I   is insides imploding thingether

melancholy of watching a coastline recede   or   the desires sublimate

into topping or bottoming or activism   inside an unspeakable noise

ever so slightly   to come

a continual   WYD?   as waters rise   colony collapses

but no no   wait what have I done   did we do   am I doing

beyond looking   endlessly   NMU?

here I is in the every wild   but of no interest in being interesting

apocalypse continues to arrive   no beginningful

and morning   mourning

In those towns on the Gulf   levies with walls on top

burst and water flows from one space into another

big tank or small pond or reasonably large field   we are in the water

up to our ankles   then knees   water rushes   rounds fallen pylons

affluent and runoff and contamination   waves on the body

of water   flows in ground mushes   like an icing   frothy frosting

you two suddenly there   a blue-bandanna

tent stitched by hand   rituals always about to take place   inside cool and pleasant

the comfort in the swirling waters

An urge to connect and to please   Urgent to break open

organic to whatever is put thingether   what floats on air

what is incorrect or impassive or ugly   what if I leans into the ugly gerunds

participles   particles   i mean ing ing ing

sometimes noun sometimes verb or adjective   names slip back and forth

what is ugly   ugly what moors   is mooring   or not ugly at all   remade

static and passiving   an object   Oh the tunnel through

a changed   historicity   a sense of I's fictions

to slice   coastline   seven cuts through the barrier island

the racket of repeated horizons

An I to undo I's sublimating

Hey   Look!   The inside linoleum   under the water

a pre-lover   When one arrives   one arrives with the desire for something

but translating here   because I is alive in the space

and I wonders what I keeps showing up for

lap after lap on the track   round and round

as Austin High School was first built

blocks from the small brick house for Hertha   and then the school's

added on to in the seventies or eighties   helicopters and white flight

and white returns   rebirths multiple

and now that addition demolished and begone!

and in the process of a rebuild for a new century

obvious spraypaint   and   quote "when this is all over"

et cetera   dust   bleek and creekless

iceballs litter   trunk   roots

unexpected   feeling   unwitnessed   who cares bitch

oweee!   you and me won't last

through the end of this century

a frightening fact   or comforting   but I wills

some sentences to string thingether

to make some thing cohere   generationally

is an ugly adverb   adverbs often deemed ugly

provide some testimony

how joining occurred   a joining

at different points with a transgressive

flare   but also tragic

or never actually happening

Lookn is an experience for an I who delights in pleasing   the eyes point away from self

abjection always available   subjection endlessly alluring   offers catharsis

a subspace of   thank you   I is just lookn   next   a Catholic search for

seething   always I to be wrong

Wrongness a turn-on   overly overtly seductive

The feeling of being ripped a new asshole   so to speak

if the one doing it   is on some level responsible   gentle   is it better

to love the fallen   to project I's voice across an expanse of hardwood floors

voice re-articulating years ago   I to stand in that power of projection

you're so defensive   she said   It's a tangle   a sub-

terranean bottom of this   of this old genealogical tree

of course there is a disconnect   if I learns

not to begin a sentence   with I   but never learned   but

always starts a defense

As if there is a way to avoid the hurricane   look!   drive around it honey

As if words were missing   or images were not seen   an image is an other abstraction

another poet does it better than I   surely   or did

oh the whipping   bring on the whipping

non-narrative and non-literary into a glistening transitional   future still imagining ing ing these potential reliquaries of so-called Texas saints

just another way of saying the same thing   the song goes

"I could build me a castle of memories"

and the songwords reverberate through the speaker

"Just to have somewhere to go"

after the conversation as I sits there

a chapel of white walls   Spanish moss and begonia

over the levee   Border Patrol rolls   Oh   friend

friendship is that   unravelling   like the passing of a grandmother

is necessary though   your insides are raising   an ineffable racket

a poetry   deeply invested in an elsewhere

and I is never quite belonging

so many I's all at once   a past I and a current eye with different tags applied

I re-reads old texts   looking for the word looking   to try to find what I is looking for

yet the same body   older yes   but same

a chapel of sorts   something misknown and pleasant

I has always thought the choir should meet every Sunday

to read each other poems   and some of that energy arrived

and with that energy   I walks outside

recuts and repots the spiraling

begonia

its caudexes

its rhizomes

coiling to exit the pot   I repots

I calls them a precarious

longing to grow through looking

and the report

I never quite arrives   but I lingers on the horizon

                and I looks out into the horizon to wonder about

                how elsewhere might arrive   we

was at home all along   I is Dorothy   goes looking too

                    love breaks in the brack

                                    I calls them ancestors   descendants

                                    licks   their

                                        empty spaces
                        and files   tongue
                                        sharp

                                    as blazing
                                        blade

Acknowledgements

Thanks to the editors who published bits of the manuscript: Alicia Wright at *Annulet: A Journal of Poetics*, Anselm Berrigan at *The Brooklyn Rail*, TC Tolbert at *Poem-a-Day*, Leslie Contreras Schwartz at *Rupture*, Noah Ross at *Bæst: A Journal of Queer Forms & Affects*, and Rebekah Smith at *What a Time to Be Alive*. Thanks to Lawndale Art Center for supporting the publication of the chapbooks *Hooks* (2019) and *Swamps Fly* (2021). And thanks to Maria Miranda Maloney of Mouthfeel Press for deciding to publish this book in its entirety.

To the hosts of the spaces where I worked on writing the pieces that eventually came to form this book (especially on Zoom during quarantine): a Frankpo Workshop by Kenji Liu, The World We Want by Aurora Masum-Javed, The Freedom in the Constraint through Woodland Pattern Book Center by TC Tolbert, Letters to the Land through Tierra Narrative by mónica teresa ortiz, Plant Perspectives through Lost in the Letters workshop by Janice Lee, Writing from the Chakras by Minal Hajratwala, a Southerners on New Ground (SONG) Race Traitors Organizing Zoom call, Literatura con álbumes familiares through Casa Octavia by Yolanda Segura, Polyphonic Intersubjectivities through Liminal Lab by Janice Lee & Elæ Moss.

To all the interlocutors who aided me as I worked on this book and the larger project of *The Unsettlements*, of which this book is one piece. Lastly, thank you to everyone organic and inorganic who helped me or loved me or supported me, especially those whose names are not here or who resist naming.

About

JD Pluecker works with language, that is, a material thing, a thing of life and history. Her undisciplinary work inhabits the intersections of writing, history, translation, art, interpreting, bookmaking, queer/trans aesthetics, non-normative poetics, language justice, and cross-border cultural production. They have translated numerous books from the Spanish, including *Antígona González* (Les Figues Press, 2016), *Trash* by Sylvia Aguilar Zéleny (Deep Vellum Press, 2023) and *In Defense of Common Life: The Political Thought of Raquel Gutiérrez Aguilar* (Common Notions, 2024). JD's book of poetry and image, *Ford Over*, was released in 2016 from Noemi Press, and in 2019 Lawndale Art Center supported the publication of the artist book, *The Unsettlements: Dad*. From 2010-2020, she worked as part of the transdisciplinary collaborative Antena Aire and from 2015-2020 with the local social justice interpreting collective Antena Houston. JD edits chapbooks with Ugly Duckling Presse's Señal series, is a recipient of the Andy Warhol Foundation Arts Writing Grant, and has exhibited work at Blaffer Art Museum, the Hammer Museum, Project Row Houses, and more. More info at www.jdpluecker.com and www. antenaantena.org.